Hugh Can Do

Hugh Can Do

BY Jennifer Armstrong

ILLUSTRATED BY Kimberly Bulcken Root

CROWN PUBLISHERS, INC.

New York

For my brother, John
—K. B. R.

Text copyright © 1992 by Jennifer M. Armstrong
Illustrations copyright © 1992 by Kimberly Bulcken Root

All rights reserved. No part of this book may be reproduced or transmitted in any form
or by any means, electronic or mechanical, including photocopying, recording, or by
any information storage and retrieval system, without permission in writing from
the publisher.

Published by Crown Publishers, Inc., a Random House company,
225 Park Avenue South, New York, New York 10003

CROWN is a trademark of Crown Publishers, Inc.

Manufactured in Hong Kong

Library of Congress Cataloging-in-Publication Data
Armstrong, Jennifer, 1961–
Hugh can do / Jennifer Armstrong ; illustrations by Kimberly Bulcken Root.
p.   cm.
Summary: Hugh wants to seek his fortune in the city, but first he
must find a way to pay the toll-taker at the bridge.
[1. Perseverance (Ethics)—Fiction.]   I. Root, Kimberly Bulcken, ill.
II. Title.
PZ7.A73367Hu   1992
[E]—dc20   90-46275
ISBN 0-517-58218-X (trade)
0-517-58219-8 (lib. bdg.)
10 9 8 7 6 5 4 3 2 1   First Edition

$\mathcal{T}$here once was a young orphan fellow named Hugh, as poor as a rabbit but as quick as a fox. He traveled for days and dreamed of his fortune, and how he would make it, and where, and how soon.

He scampered and skipped and he dawdled and
dallied, and stopped for a rest on the bank of a river.
Scooping a handful of water to drink, he saw in the
distance the towers and streets of a great shining
city.

"In a city like that, a fellow
like me can certainly make
his way," he said.

He stood by the river
and peered up and down.

Far to his left was an old wooden bridge at the
edge of a village. Without waiting a second,
Hugh ran down to cross it.

But when he arrived, a big, burly Tollbooth Man barred his way. "Hold on there, young Sprout. Where to now, so fast and so fiery?"

"I'm crossing this bridge, sir, to get to the city and hatch up my fortune. I'm in kind of a hurry, so please let me by."

"You must pay the toll," said the big, burly man. "No man crosses bridges without paying tolls."

Hugh turned out his pockets to show they were empty. "And what am I to do, then?"

The Tollbooth Man rubbed at his whiskery chin and rolled his bulgy black eyes. "Hmm, there, young Sprout. Say you get me a nice loaf of bread for my lunch. Was you to do that, why, then I'd let you cross!"

Hugh slapped his knee. "Done!" he replied, and he darted back into the village.

The yeasty brown scent of freshly baked bread led Hugh by the nose to a Baker. He ran in the door and leaned his hands on the counter.

"I'd like some bread," he announced with a smile.

The white-floured Baker pulled his head from the oven. He patted his stomach and looked young Hugh over. "Well, well, Mister Muffinhead. It'll cost you a bit."

Hugh turned out his pockets to show they were empty. "What am I to do, then?"

The Baker chomped on a cake while he thought for a spell and licked a big dollop of cream from his chin. "Say you take this here grain down the stream to the Miller. Get it ground up and sifted and bring it back here. Was you to do that, why, I'd give you a loaf."

Hugh slapped his knee. "Done! Give me your grain."

He dashed out the door and raced for the river and found the old mill with its rumbling wheel. "I need this wheat ground, and I need it done fast," he said, dumping the sack on the grain-covered floor.

Gritting his teeth on a piece of rock candy, the Miller examined Hugh's grain with a grin. "You do, Mister Leapfrog? Well, grinding grain fine or grinding it foul, grinding grain costs more than nothing, you know."

Hugh turned out his pockets to show they were empty. "What am I to do, then?"

The Miller leaned down and peered into Hugh's eyes. "I need this here apron sewn up with fine stitches." He pulled his torn apron off over his head. "Say you get these here rips sewn up nice as a hanky. Was you to do that, why, I'd grind you your grain. I'd grind it up fine, and I'd grind it up fast."

Hugh slapped his knee. "Done! Give me your apron."

He raced from the mill and back into the village. Above a small shop swung a big spool of thread. "Here's the Tailor," Hugh said, bounding in like a hare.

"I need this apron fixed! I need it fast," he cried, swinging it down on the Tailor's big table.

"So, Mister Ripsnorter. You need my services? You need my help?" The Tailor took hold of the tattered old apron, and looked young Hugh up and then looked young Hugh down. "I won't do it for nothing, lad. I've got to eat."

Hugh turned out his pockets to show they were empty. "What am I to do, then?"

The Tailor sat down and crossed his long legs. "I fancy some goose eggs to eat for my supper. A dozen will do. If you bring 'em here, then I'll needle this apron as fast as a hummingbird."

Hugh slapped his knee. "Done!"

He skipped out the door and down to the meadow. "Hey, Goosegirl," he yelled as he charged through her flock. "I've need of some eggs! A dozen will do!"

The Goosegirl was twirling her curls with her hand, and she looked young Hugh up and then looked young Hugh down. "Oh, you do, Wild-Goose Chaser? And maybe you think that twelve goose eggs come free?"

Hugh turned out his pockets to show they were empty. "What am I to do, then?"

The Goosegirl picked up a gray goose in her arms. She ruffled its feathers and frowned while she thought.

"There's a wizened old witch who lives down by the river. I want a love charm, so get it from her. Say you bring me a love charm, why, you'd have your eggs."

Hugh slapped his knee. "Done!"

He dashed through the goose flock and made for the river.

Down by the rushes and weedy green banks, young Hugh found a cottage and banged on the door. "Witch lady, come on out! Spin me a charm!"

A shrivelly crone poked her head out the window. "So, young Potato! You're daring to ask me?"

Hugh folded his arms and he nodded his head. "Certainly, madam. I've need of your services! I want a love charm to give to the Goosegirl to get me some eggs to give to the Tailor to mend an old apron to give to the Miller to grind up some flour to take to the Baker to get a fresh loaf to give as a bridge toll. And I can't say plainer than that."

"No sir, young master. But first you must give to me something of value."

Hugh turned out his pockets to show they were empty. "What am I to do, then?"

The wrinkly witch threw her head back and chuckled. She cracked all her knuckles and danced on her toes. "Bring to me that which I value the most, and you, lad, shall have what you ask!"

The window slammed shut with a bang in Hugh's face, and he wandered away to sit by the river. Off in the distance, the flags of the city beckoned and waved and saluted to Hugh. He wrinkled his forehead and scratched at his feet, trying to think what the witch could desire.

"Come now, young Hugh. You can do it," he scolded. "A lonely old witch should be easy to please.

"But what could she value? What makes her smile? She's an expert at magic, a champion of charms. What could she want that she can't whistle up? What could she need that young Hugh can supply?"

He frowned and he scowled and
grimaced and squinted and chewed on
his thumbnail and pulled on his ear.

"Think now, Hugh, think!" he said,
snapping his fingers. "She's welcome to all
that I have if she wants it, but all that
I've got is myself. It's not much."

But the more he considered,
the more he decided he had
something fine.

"Aha!" Hugh exclaimed. "I've got it! I'm sure!" He scampered on back to the old witch's cottage and kicked on the door with the toe of his shoe.

"Hello! It's me, Hugh! I've done what you asked me!"

The window flew open. The witch crone looked out.

"Young Potato! Have you brought to me something of value?"

Hugh slapped his knee. "Done!"

He held out his hand and gave her a smile. "This is my offer. Here's what I have. My friendship, a handshake, and help when you ask. I'm as poor as a rabbit but willing to share."

"Oho, young Potato! That's all that you've got? Your friendship? A handshake? A promise to care?"

The witch gave a snort and let out a laugh, and leaned out the window and spoke in Hugh's ear.

"You're sure now, Potato? That's your half of the deal?"

"I'm sure," he said.

"Fine!" the witch cried. "Now that there's what I call a wonderful gift! The one single treasure I hope for each day! I finally have it! So here is your love charm. It's paid up in full!"

She tossed out a bottle and waved at young Hugh. "Now don't be a stranger! Hurry back soon!" She slammed shut the window and left Hugh alone.

"Oho!" cried Hugh as he picked up the bottle. "Now here's where we get started!"

He ran back to the meadow and chased down the Goosegirl. "Here you go! Now for my eggs!"

"Take them as you please," the Goosegirl replied with a dimply smile.

Hugh picked up twelve goose eggs and ran to the Tailor.

"Here you go! Now for my apron!"

"All mended as good as new," said the Tailor with a needly grin.

Hugh picked up the apron and ran to the Miller.

"Here you go! Now for my flour!"

"Ground as fine as diamond dust," said the Miller with a grating laugh.

Hugh picked up the flour and ran to the Baker.

"Here you go! Now for my bread!"

"Baked as hot as a coal," said the Baker with a dusty sneeze.

Hugh picked up the bread and ran to the bridge.

"Here you go! Now let me pass!"

A scraggy old man hobbled out of the tollbooth.

"Hold on there, young Skidder. Where to, so hot and happy, your bread in your fist?"

Hugh spun around and gaped at the man. "Where's the big, burly Tollbooth Man? Where has he gone to? I brought him my toll!"

The scraggy old man cackled high, chuckled low. "What, the bread? Be off with you, Skidder. Don't waste my time. I'm the Number Two Toll Man, and I don't take bread!"

With a snap of his fingers he hopped back inside.

"What am I to do *now*?" Frowning and fuming and rubbing his nose, Hugh sat by the tollbooth and chomped on the bread.

"I played by the rules. I did what they asked me. But now that I'm finished they've changed the whole game!" He nibbled and frowned and he pondered and chewed till his loaf was no more than a pile of crumbs.

"And now I'm right back where I started! Empty pockets as bare as a bone and no way to cross this rickety bridge! I can't reach the city and make my own way."

"Hugh!" wheezed a voice.

"Hey, Hugh!" called a rough one.

"Um, Hugh," hemmed another.

"Yoo-hoo!" cooed a fourth.

He sprang to his feet and whooped with surprise. "The Baker! The Miller! The Tailor! The Goosegirl! Where are you going all crammed in a wagon?"

"We're off to the city," the Baker replied. "And if you can squeeze in, you're welcome to come. One toll for one wagon, and we've got that here. You've dealt with us fairly, and we're glad to share!"

Hugh slapped his knee and let out a laugh. "Done!" he cried, and hopped on the wagon.

The wagon moved forward. The Toll Man popped out. His long pointed nose sniffled left, sniffled right. He held out one hand and tip-tapped one long foot.

"Your toll," said the Tailor, and flipped him a coin. "And now let us get on our way, if you please."

The wooden boards rumbled. The river slid past. The Goosegirl sang love songs, and Hugh crossed the bridge. He peered down the stream as they trundled across, and saw the old witch by her cottage.

"I'll be back!" Hugh promised, and stood up to wave.

The witch blew a kiss, which Hugh put in his pocket, and he settled back down with a smile. Ahead was the road to the great shining city, and Hugh knew, for certain, his fortune was made.